Mom's Shoes

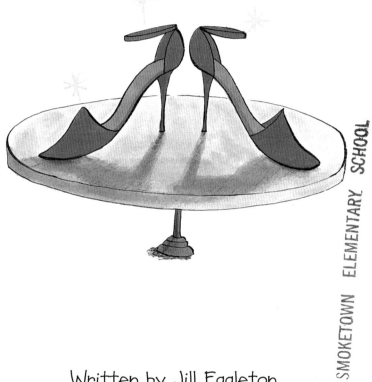

Written by Jill Eggleton
Illustrated by Helen Bacon

Rigby

On Saturday,
Mom and I went shopping.
"I'm going to get some new shoes,"
said Mom.

"You have tons of shoes," I said.

"I want some shoes with high heels," said Mom.

3

We went into the shoe store,
and the man got out boxes of shoes.
Mom saw some shoes with **very** high heels.
"I like these," she said.

"You can't walk in shoes like that," I said.
"Yes, I can," said Mom.

Mom went
wobble, wobble, wobble
all over the store!

"You are walking like a duck," I said.

"I like walking like a duck," said Mom.

"You look silly," I said, but Mom didn't care.

Mom gave the man some money.
"You can put my old shoes
in the trash," she said.
"I'll wear my new shoes home."

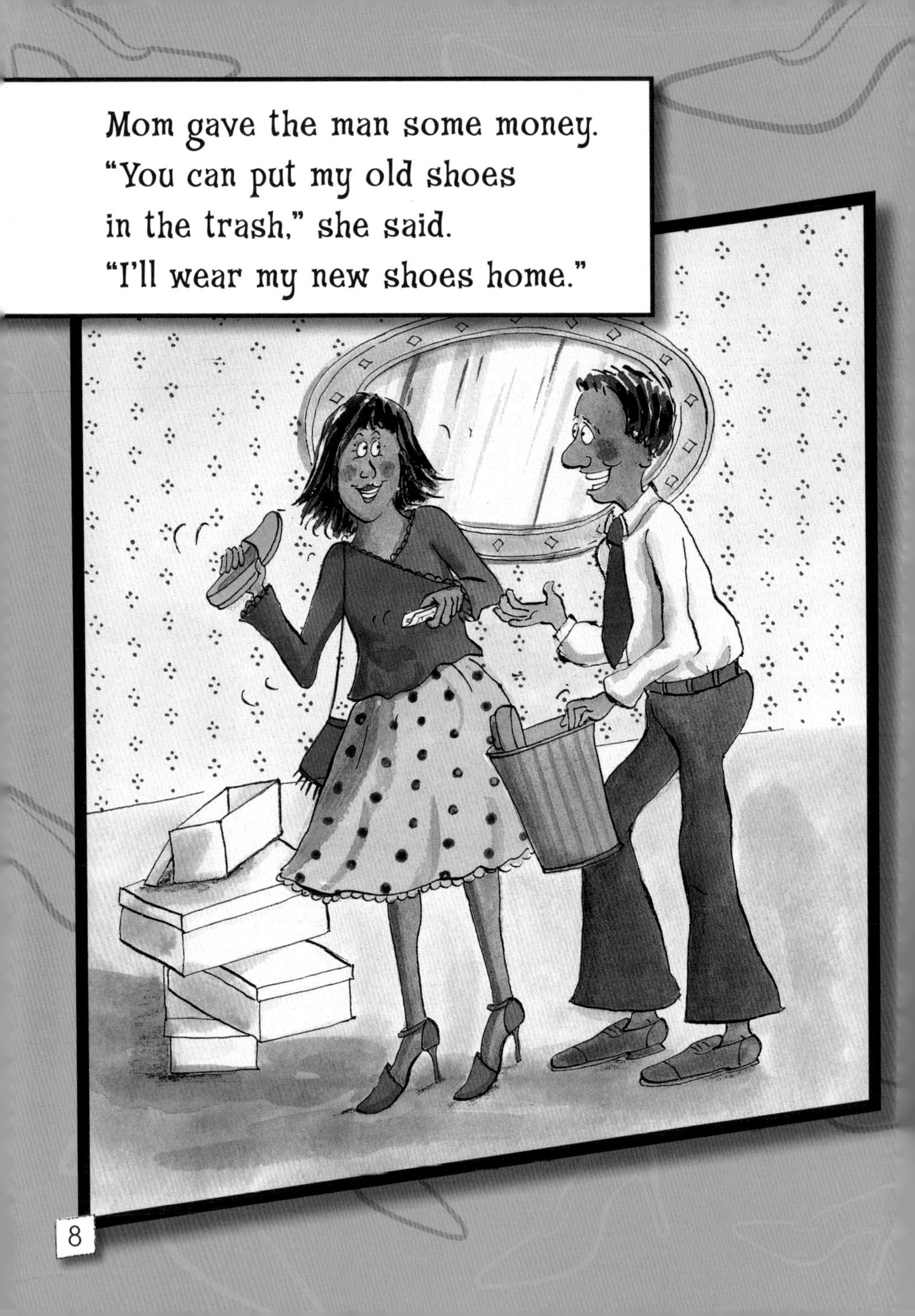

Mom went

wobble, wobble, wobble

out of the store!

Then she went

wobble, wobble, wobble

onto the escalator.

When the escalator went down,
I got off, but Mom didn't.

"Get off!" I shouted.

"I can't," said Mom.
"My shoe is stuck."

A man had to come
and stop the escalator.
Everyone was staring at us.

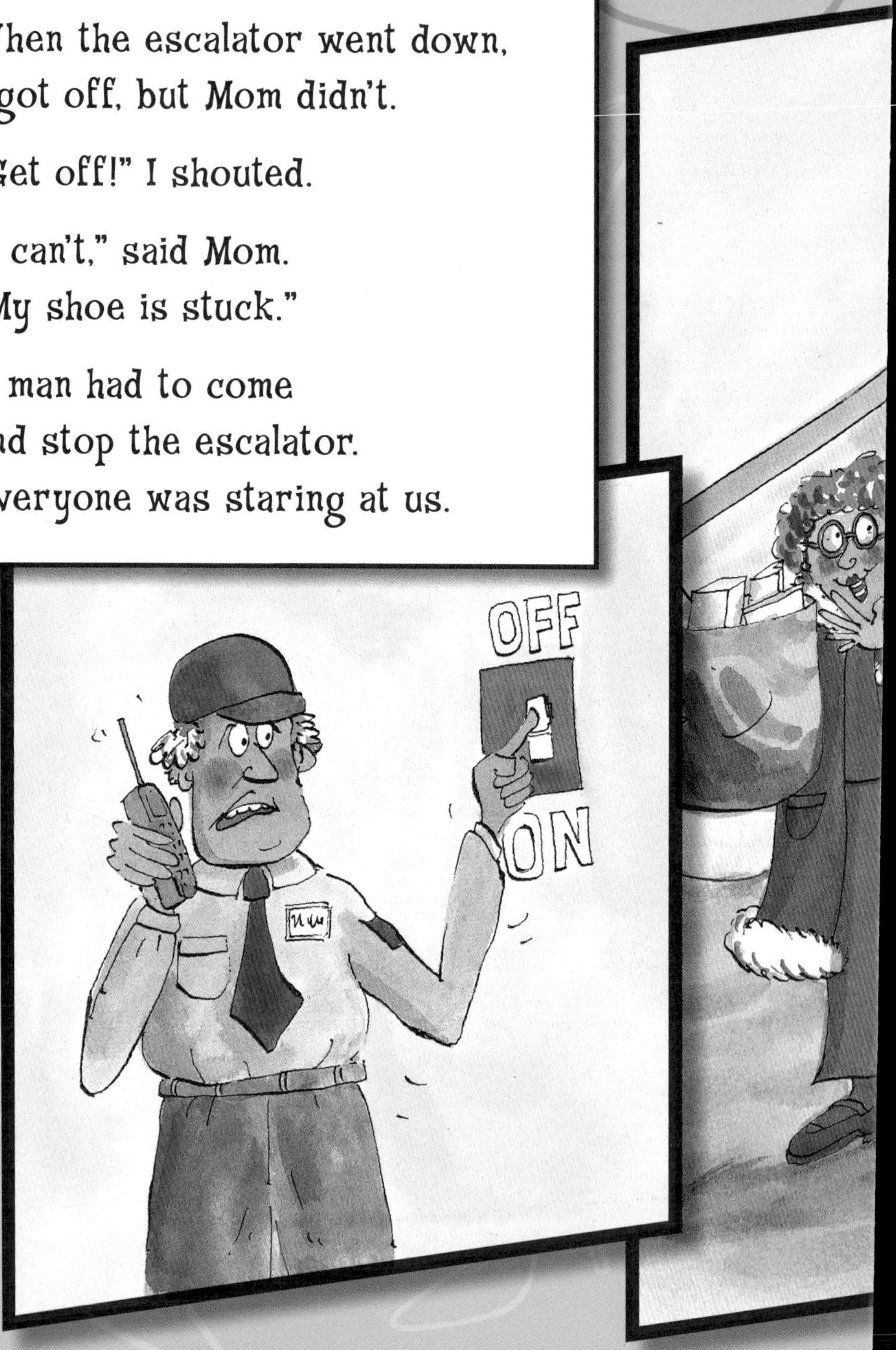
OFF
ON

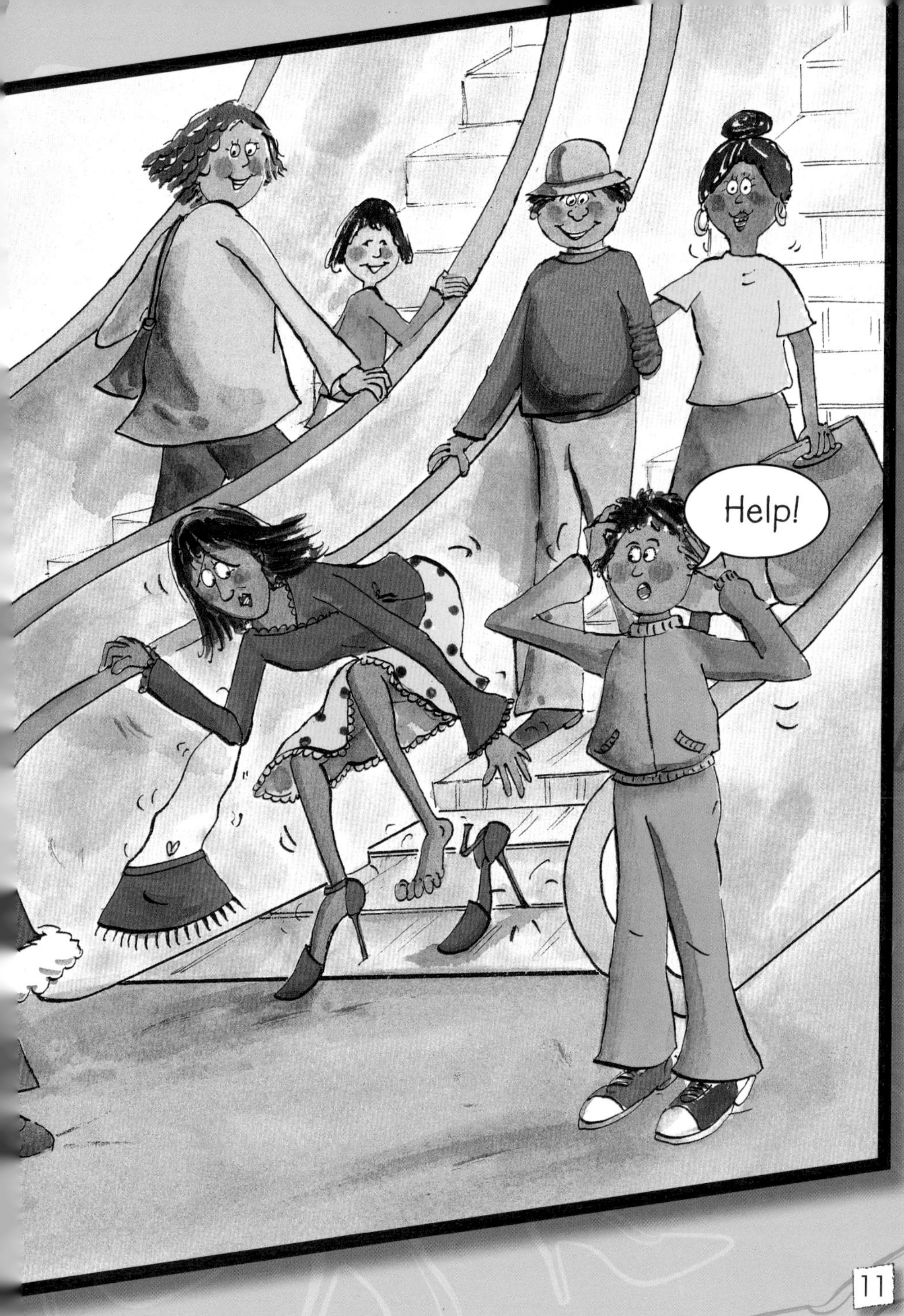
Help!

Mom went
wobble, wobble, wobble
down the street.

Her shoes went
clack, clack, clack.
"You sound like a train," I said.

Then Mom stopped.
"My shoe is stuck again," she said.

"Oh, no," I said.

Mom's shoe was stuck in a crack.

We pulled and pulled
and pulled and pulled.
Then **Snap**!

The shoe came out,
but the heel was still stuck in the crack.

We laughed and laughed
until we couldn't laugh anymore.

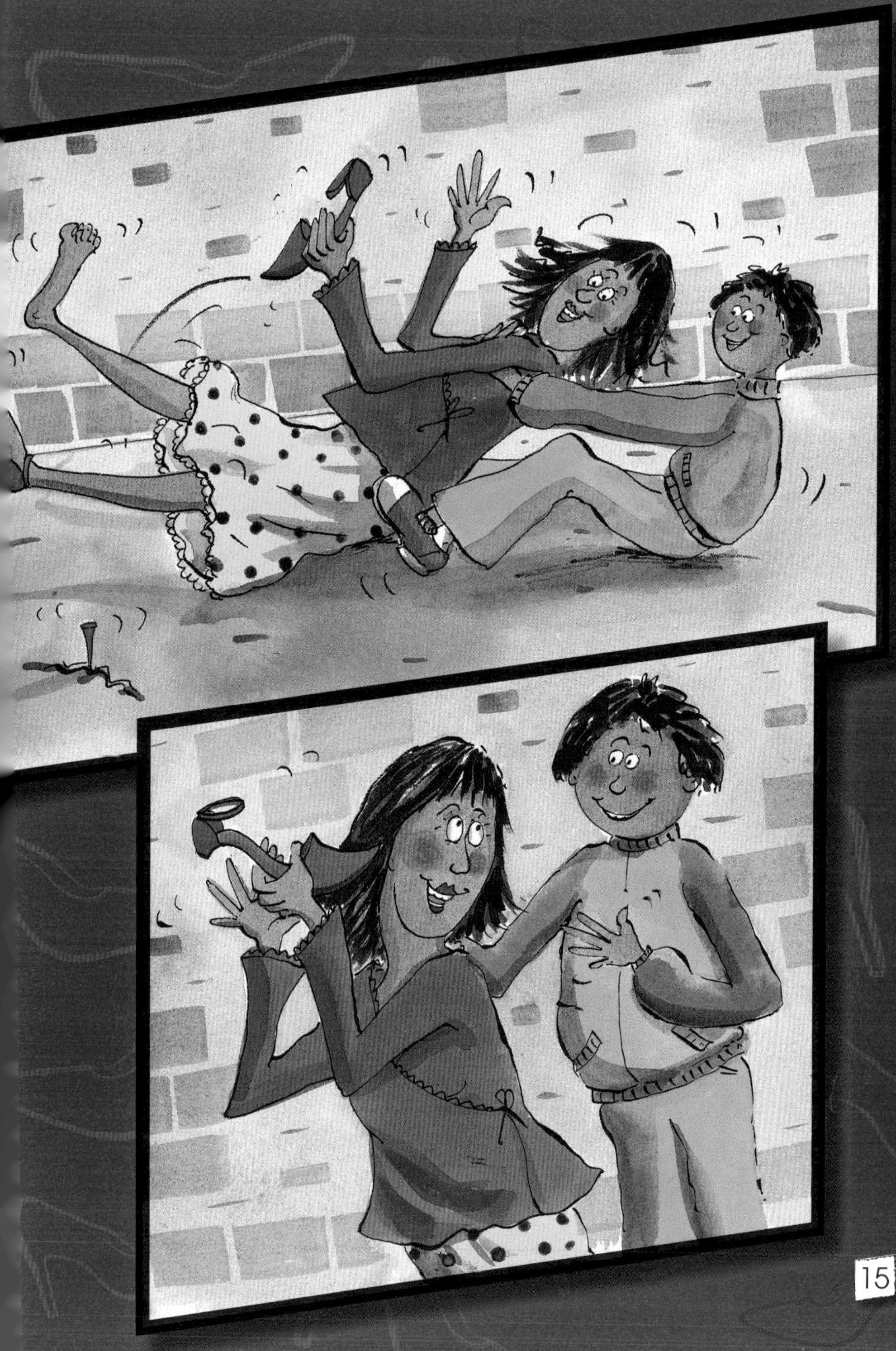

Then Mom got some newspaper
out of her bag.
"I'll make a paper shoe," she said.

Mom put on her paper shoe
and went
clack, swish, clack, swish
all the way home.

Everyone was staring,
but Mom didn't care.

Shoes! Sh

Spotty shoes, dotty shoes

Clicketty, clacketty shoes

Buy

oes! Shoes!

Clunky, chunky shoes.

Any sort of shoes.

them here!

Guide Notes

Title: Mom's Shoes

Stage: Launching Fluency – Orange

Genre: Fiction

Approach: Guided Reading

Processes: Thinking Critically, Exploring Language, Processing Information

Written and Visual Focus: Advertisement, Speech Bubbles

Word count: 298

THINKING CRITICALLY
(sample questions)

- What do you think this story could be about? Look at the title and discuss.
- Look at the cover. What sort of shoes do you think Mom likes?
- Look at pages 2 and 3. Why do you think Mom wants high-heeled shoes?
- Look at pages 4 and 5. Why do you think the boy thought that his mom couldn't walk in shoes like that?
- Look at pages 8 and 9. How do you think Mom feels about her new shoes? Why do you think that?
- Look at pages 10 and 11. How do you think the boy feels about his mom being stuck on the escalator? How do you know that?
- Look at pages 12 and 13. The boy said that his mom sounded like a train. Why do you think Mom was making such a noise?
- Look at pages 14 and 15. Mom has just broken her brand new shoe. Why do you think she is laughing?

EXPLORING LANGUAGE

Terminology
Author and illustrator credits, ISBN number

Vocabulary
Clarify: heels, escalator
Singular/Plural: shoe/shoes, heel/heels, newspaper/newspapers
Homonyms: new/knew, no/know

Print Conventions
Apostrophes – contractions (can't, didn't, I'll, I'm, couldn't), possessive (Mom's)